PENGUIN CRIME FICTION

ABRACADAVER

Peter Lovesey was born in Whitton, England, in 1936.
Educated at Reading University, he was head of the educa-
tion department at Hammersmith and West London Col-
lege until becoming a full-time writer in 1975. His crime
novels, featuring Detective Sergeant Cribb, reflect a meticu-
lous interest in Victorian social and sporting settings. Of
these, *A Case of Spirits; The Detective Wore Silk Drawers;
Mad Hatter's Holiday; Swing, Swing Together; Waxwork;*
and *Wobble to Death* are published by Penguin Books.
Peter Lovesey lives in Surrey, England, with his wife and
two children.